Lots of S

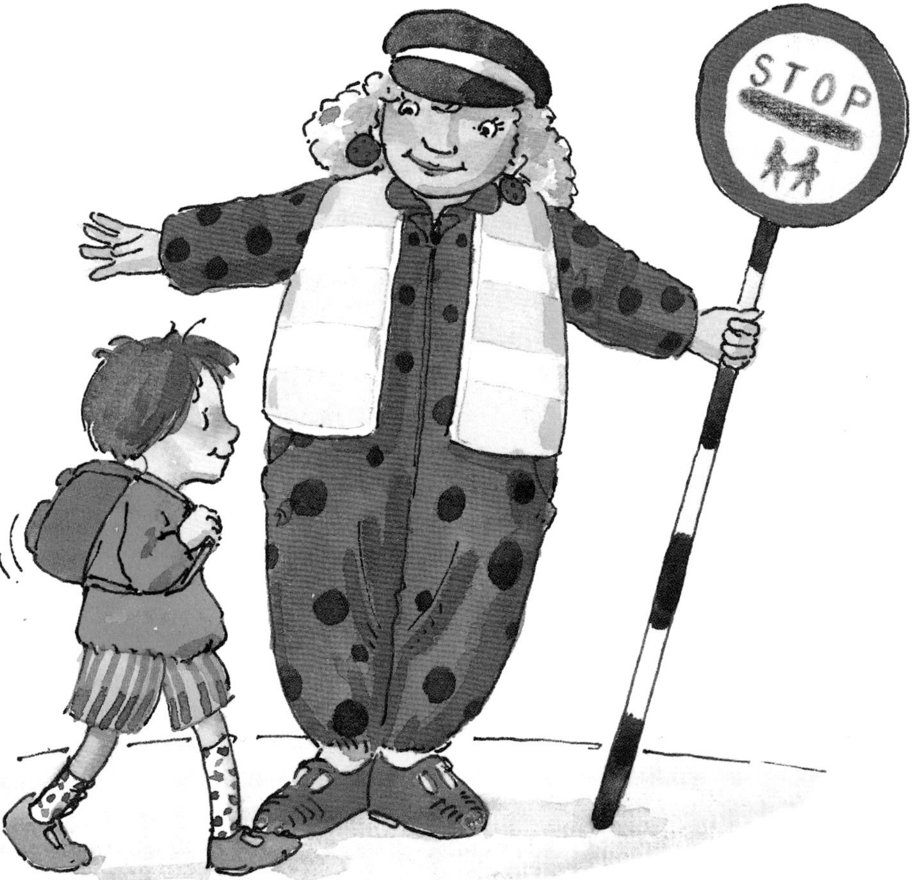

Elspeth Graham

Illustrated by Ian Newsham

OXFORD
UNIVERSITY PRESS

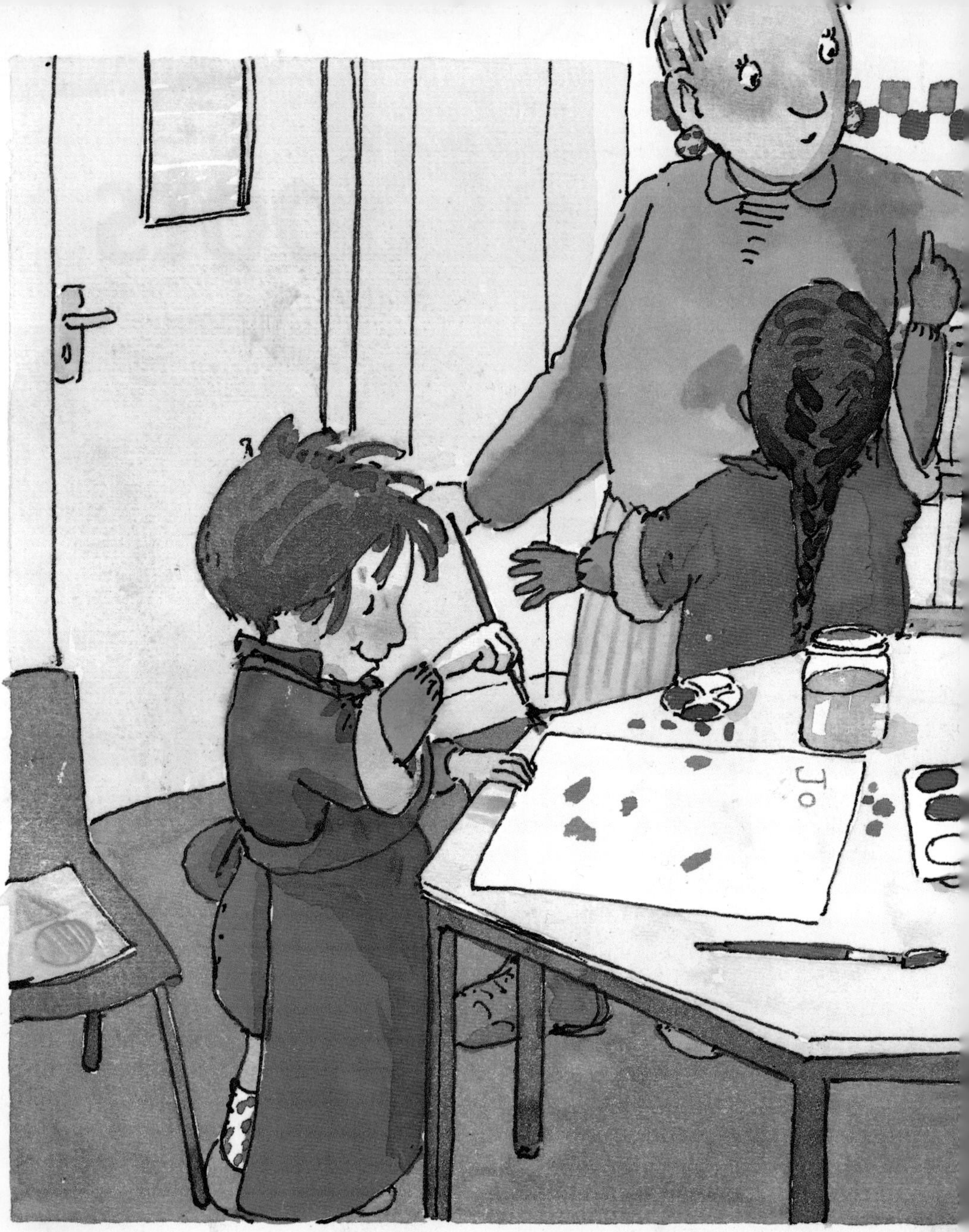

Blue spots.

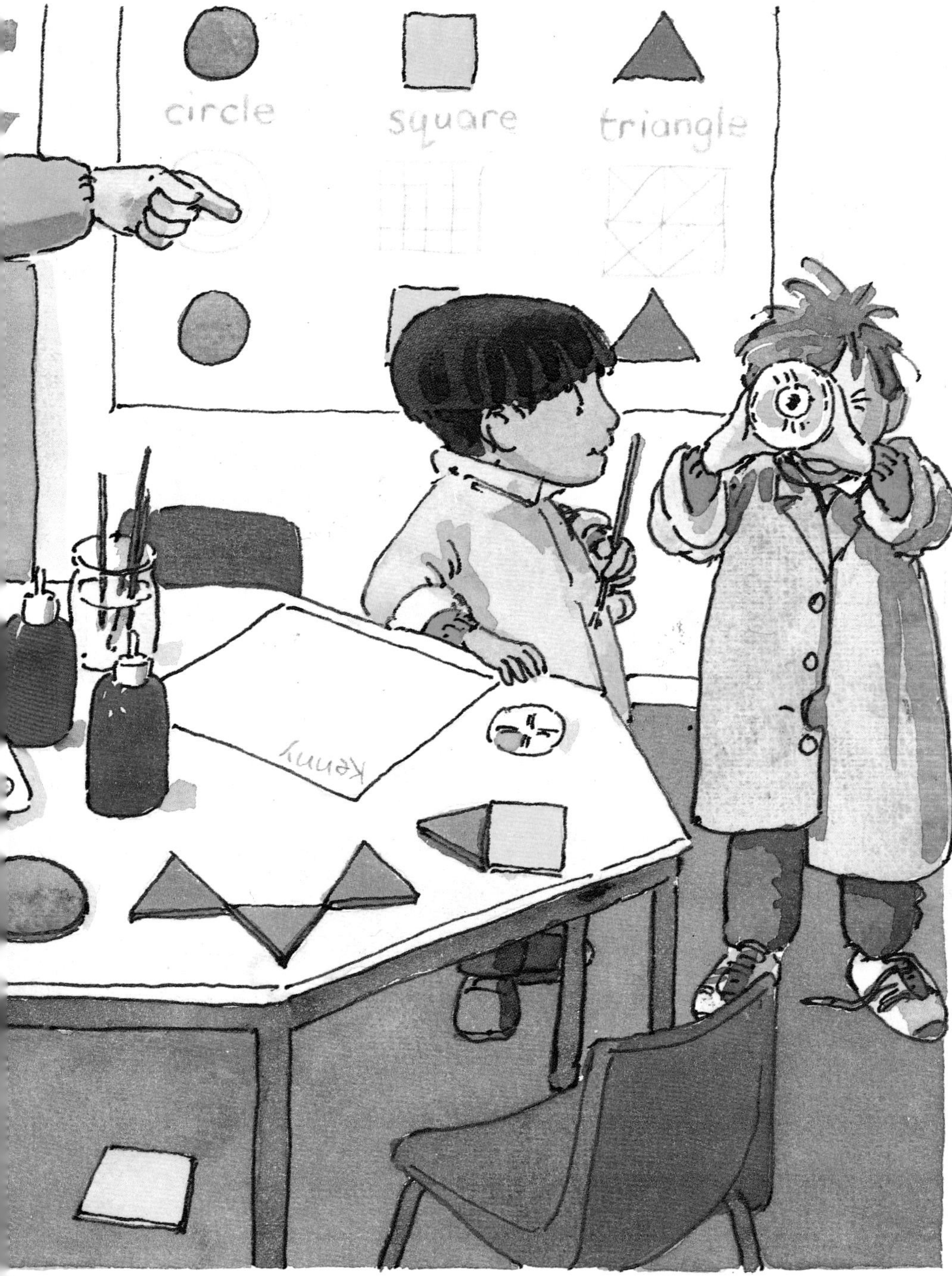
circle
square
triangle
Kenny

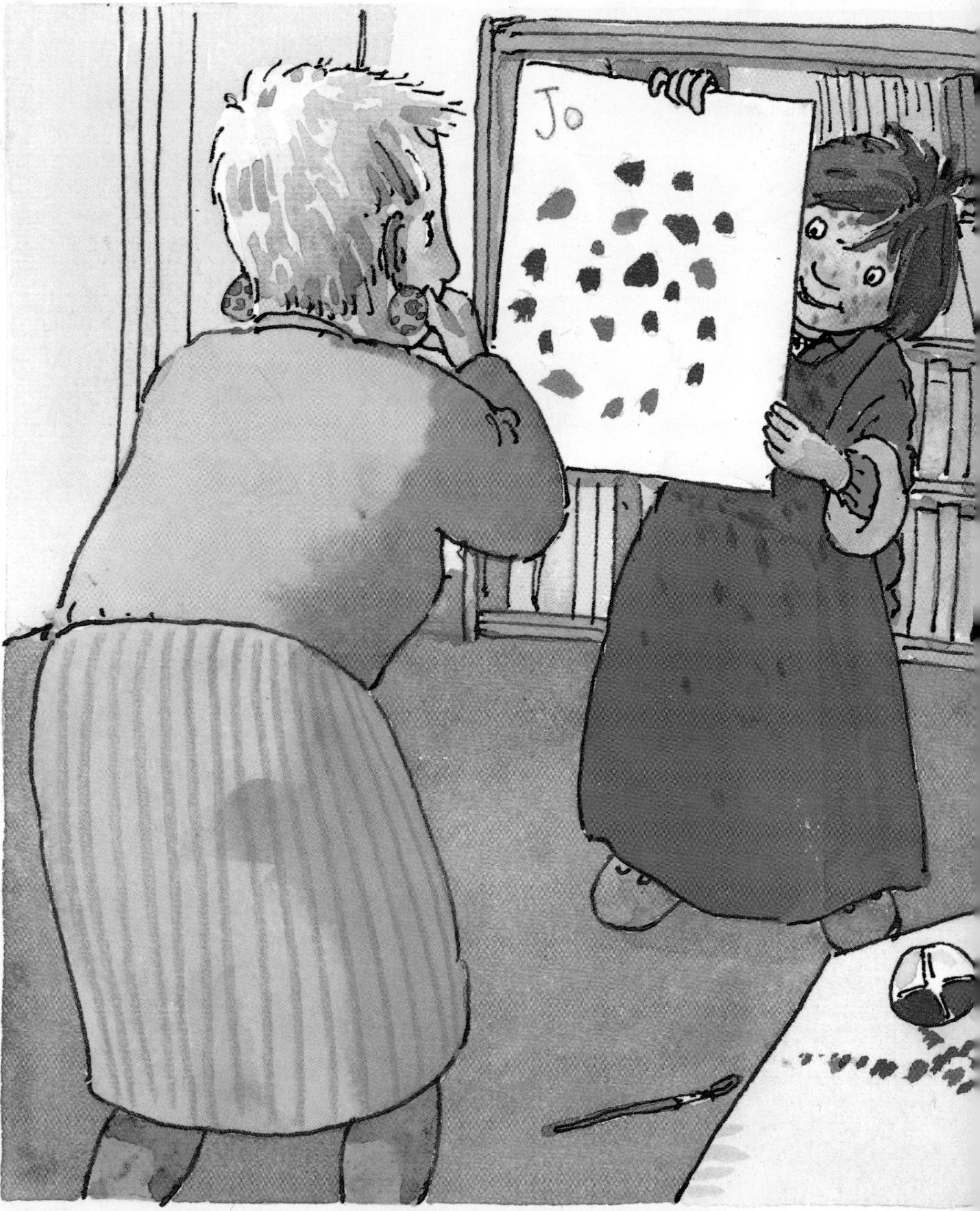

Blue and red spots.

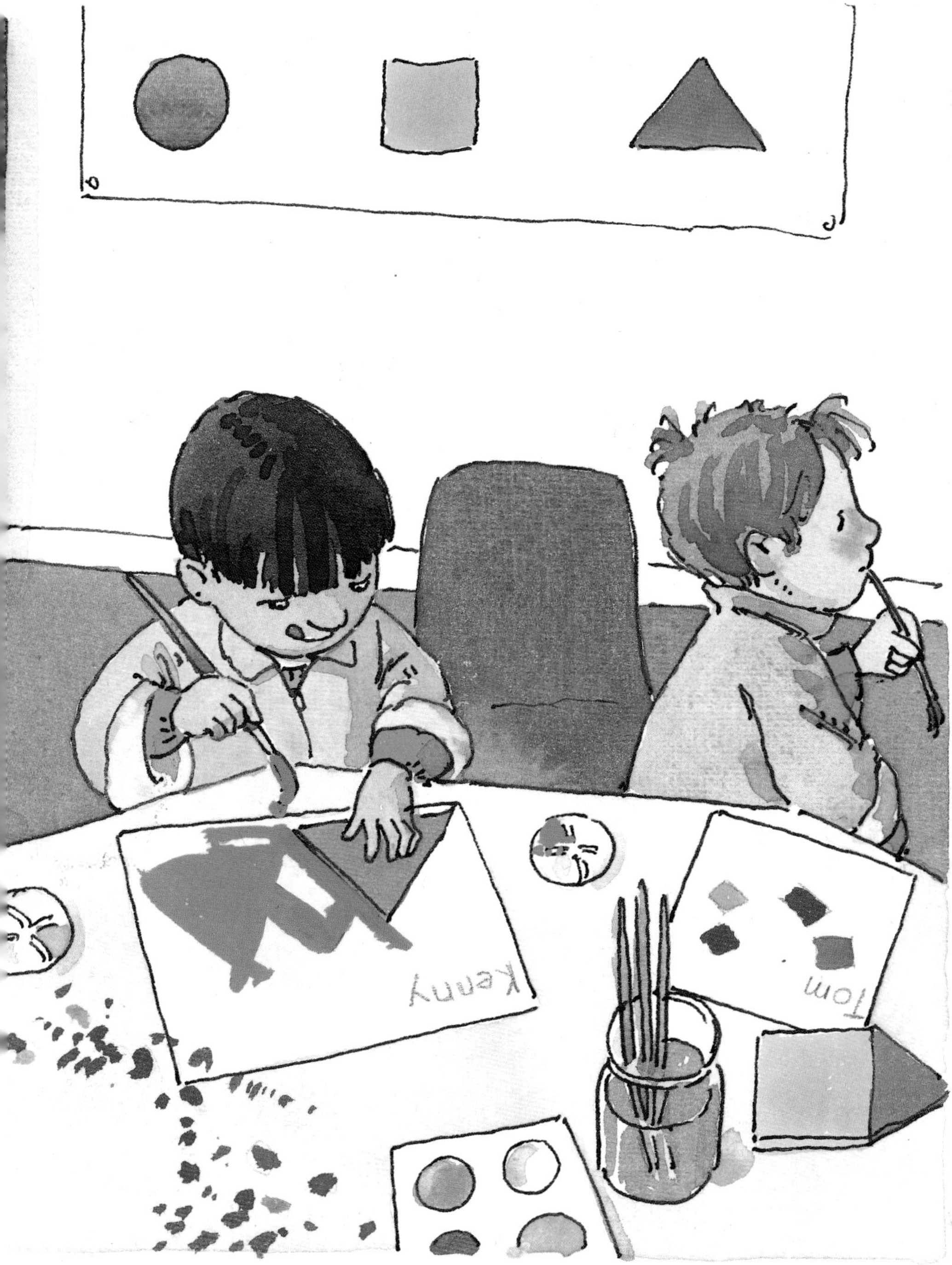
Kenny
Tom

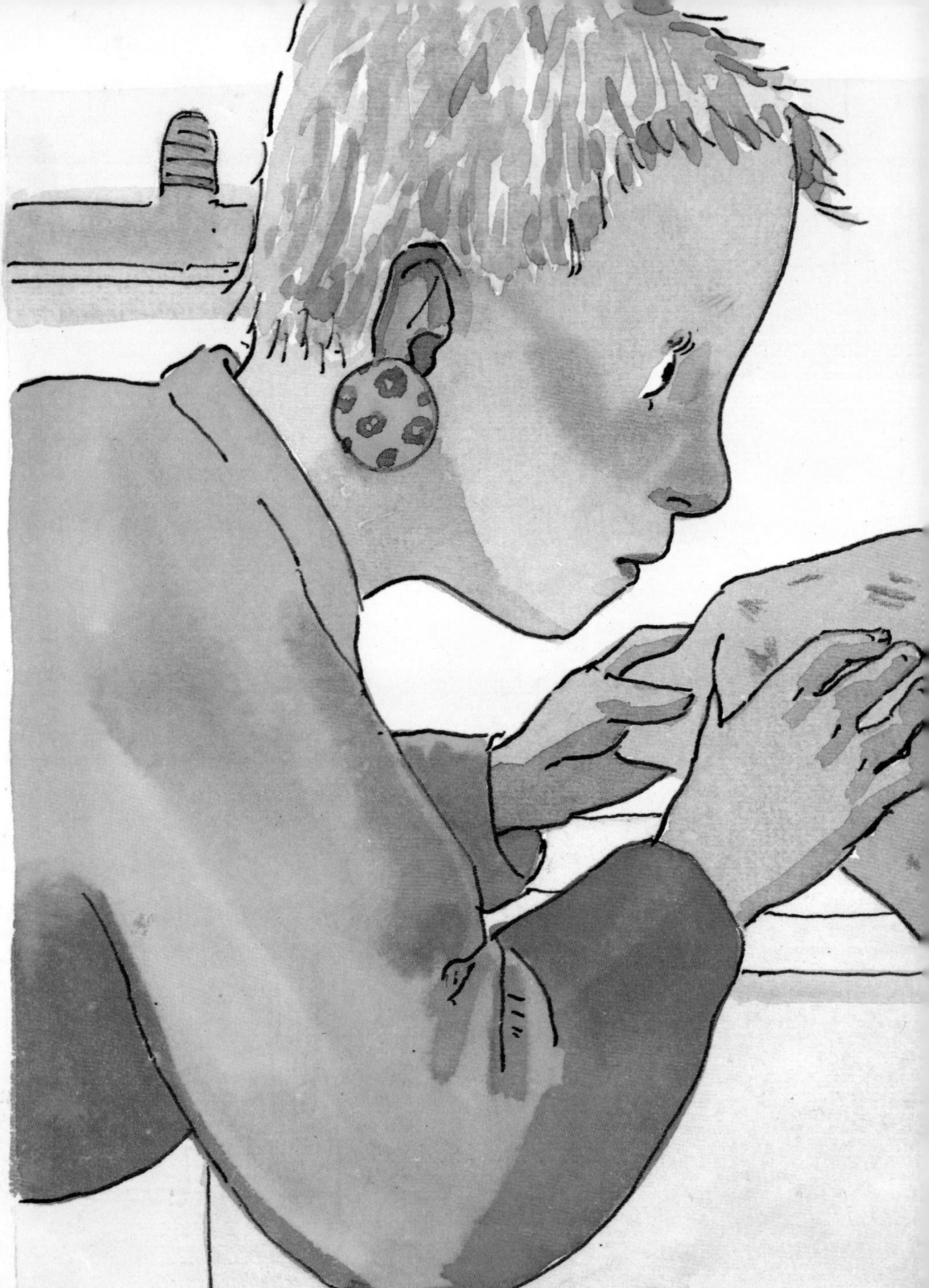

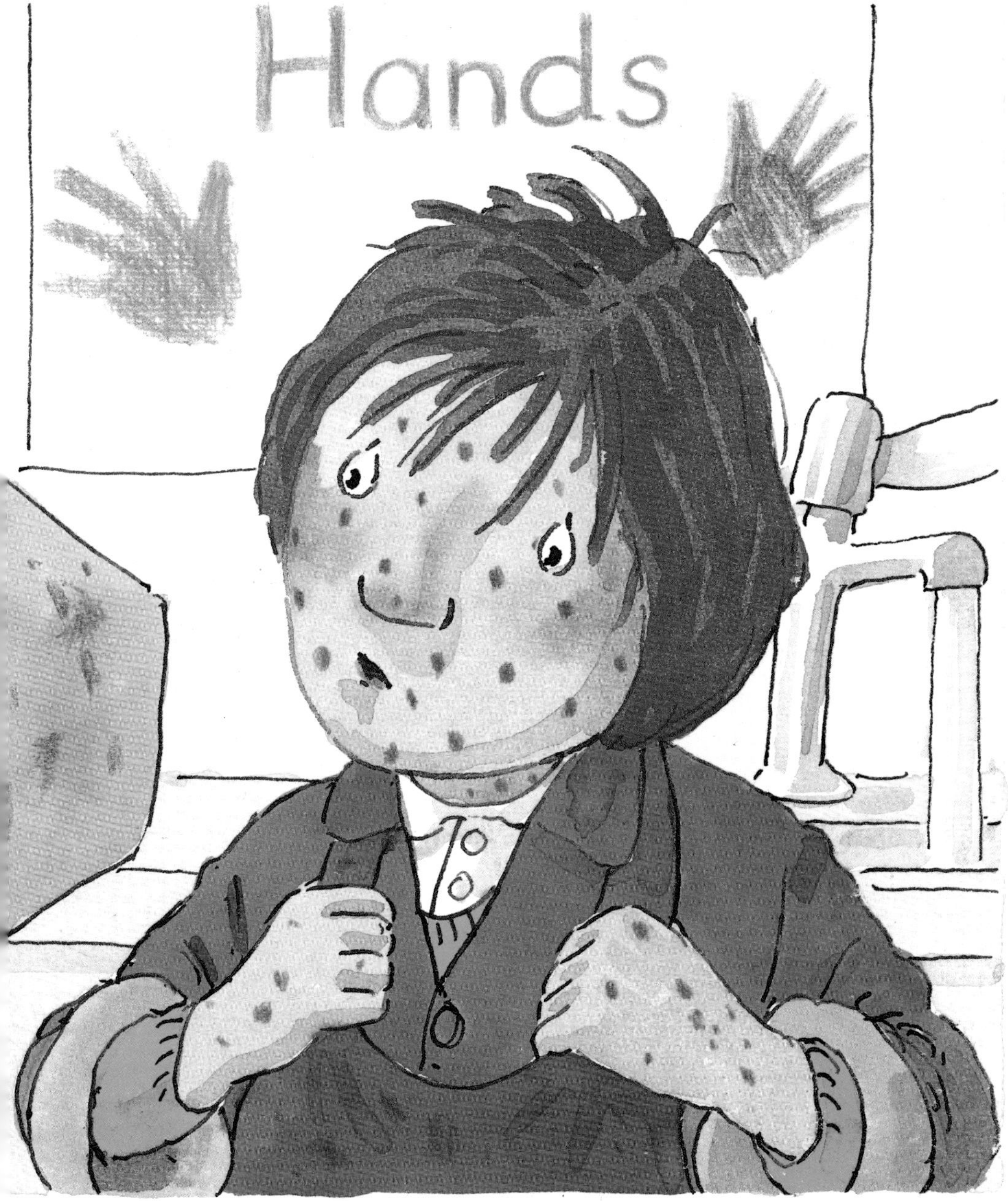

Lots of spots.

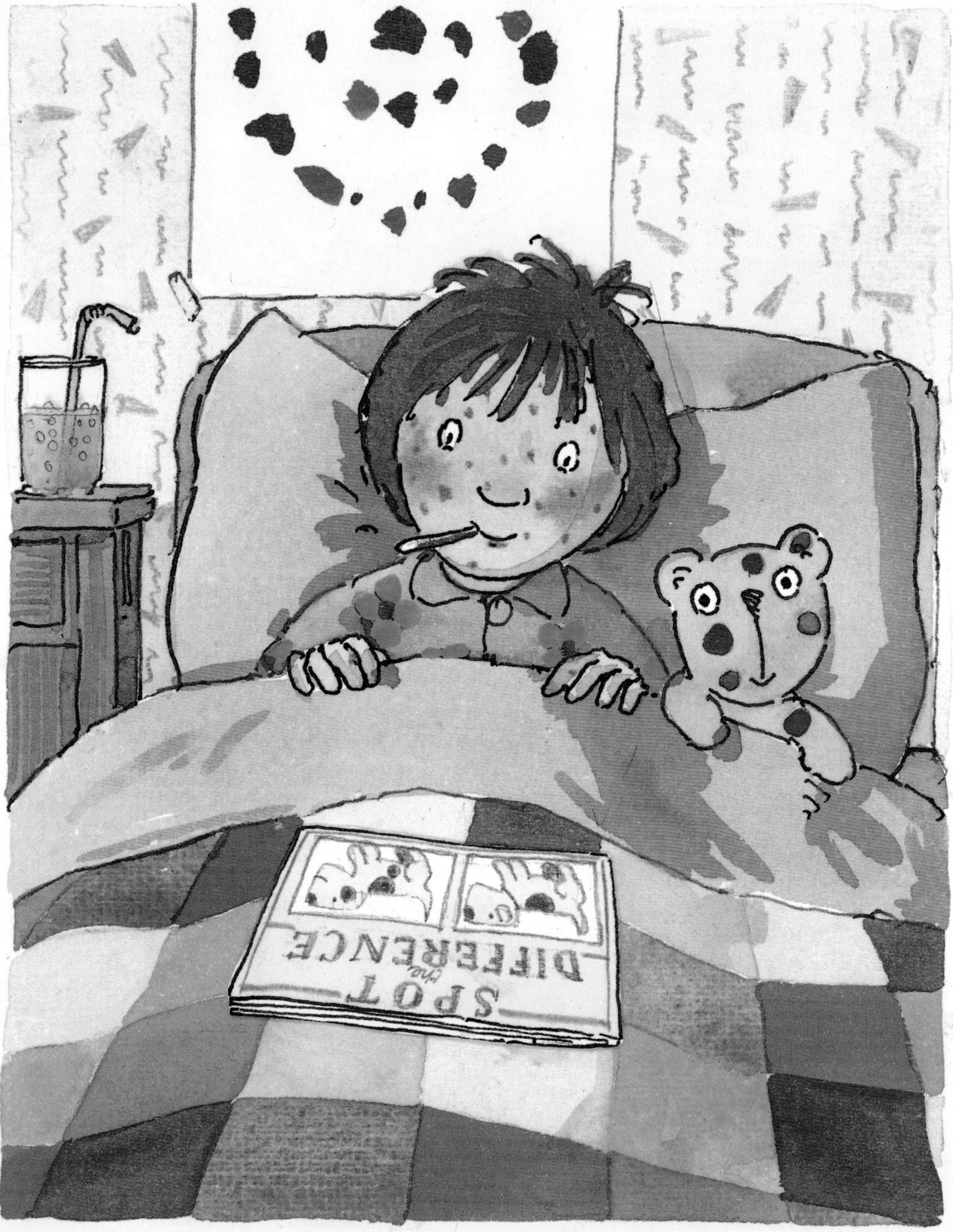

Chicken pox.